'…ripping… …zany comic
hilarious.' *Guardian* writing and
elegantly ghastly
pictures that
are a joy.'
Glasgow Herald

'Mortimer will
quickly be a real
favourite among
newly independent
readers.'
Birmingham Mail

'Fun, fast-paced
and engaging.'
South Wales Echo

'A wonderfully
inventive story,
superbly presented
and full of amazing
illustrations.'
Parents in Touch

'Humorous rhyming
text is well matched
with lively, amusing
illustrations.'
Peters Gazette

First published in 2016 by Hodder Children's Books

Text copyright © Tim Healey
Illustrations copyright © Chris Mould

Hodder Children's Books, an imprint of Hachette Children's Group, part of Hodder & Stoughton,
Carmelite House, 50 Victoria Embankment, London EC4Y 0DZ.

A catalogue record of this book is available from the British Library.

ISBN: 978 1 444 91971 4

Printed in China

An Hachette UK Company

www.hachette.co.uk

MORTIMER KEENE

KEENE

THE BEAST OF THE BAY

Tim Healey and Chris Mould

Mortimer Keene

Age: 8
Special features: specs
Weak point: none!
Favourite phrase:
'Let's give it a go.'

Sue Law

Age: 7
Special features:
loves the seaside
Weak point: doesn't
believe in sea monsters
Favourite phrase:
'I'm really looking
forward to this!'

Ronnie Ross
Age: 9
Special features: cheery face
Weak point: overconfidence
Favourite phrase: 'What could possibly go wrong?'

Wayne Ross
Age: 8
Special features: glum appearance
Weak point: negative thinking
Favourite phrase: 'I told you this would happen!'

Mrs Patel

Age: 36
Special features:
geography teacher
Weak point:
obsessed with maps
Favourite phrase:
'Where are we, exactly?'

Chief of Coastguards

Age: 48
Special features:
Very excitable
Weak point: a bit rash
Favourite phrase:
'Get out the flare guns!'

SAINT BARNABAS

S
B

SCHOOL

Darkwater
Monster

Age: unknown
Special features: long,
slithery tentacles
Weak point:
hard to get hold of
Favourite phrase:
(doesn't speak!)

Up in the science lab,
Mortimer Keene
Put a finishing touch
To his latest machine –

A new AQUAPLANE!
This cunning affair
Should work just as well
On land, sea or air.

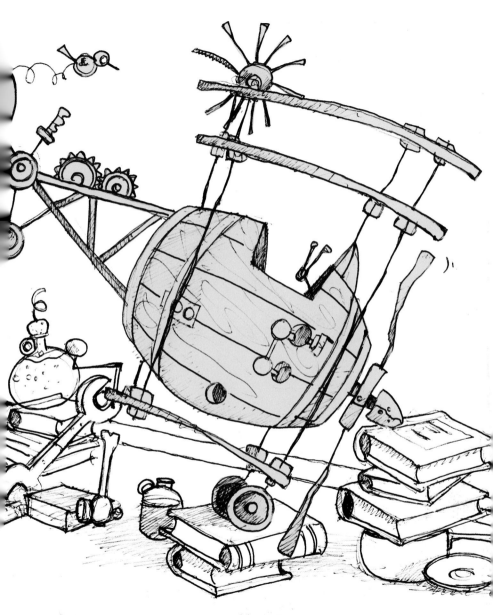

His school friends, meanwhile,
Were away for the day
On a trip, fossil-hunting
At **DARKWATER BAY.**

The weather was dismal,
And there on the sand
Stood young Mr Bevan,
With guidebook in hand.

'It's a dangerous place
With a peril besides
The risks that are posed
By the cliffs and wild tides.

It's believed that a monster
Lurks under the bay;
It has long, slimy tentacles,
So legends say.'

'We'd better be careful,'
Said Mrs MacNee,
Who was perched on a rock
With a thermos of tea.

'It's all stuff and nonsense,
And I want no part
In talk about monsters,'
Declared Mr Hart.

Little Sue Law
Was quick to agree:
'There are NO scary monsters
Out there in the sea.'

Then she yelped, 'YIKES!'
And with a start
Reeled back as a tentacle
GRABBED Mr Hart!

He wriggled and wrestled
To get himself free –
But it dragged him remorselessly
Under the sea.

He was dunked in the waves
Then whisked way up high,
And waggled around
And around in the sky.

'Call for the coastguards!'
Wailed one of the staff,
But the Beast of the Bay
Gave a horrible laugh.

24

Everyone panicked
And ran from the shore.
Then Mrs Patel cried,
'Where's little Sue Law?'

25

They stopped in their tracks
And looked back at the sea;
'The Monster has got her!'
Shrieked Mrs MacNee.

'This trip is a nightmare,'
Said Mrs Moray,
'I'll try to get Mortimer
Here to the bay.'

She got on her mobile
And swiftly began
To explain what had happened.
'COME QUICK AS YOU CAN!'

29

Mortimer paused.
Would his plane really fly?
Now was the moment
To give it a try.

'Yes!' he exclaimed,
As the plane rose with ease,
Zooming up from the school
Above houses and trees.

He called the head teacher:
'All going OK,'
And shot off like an arrow
For Darkwater Bay.

Teachers and children
Crouched low on the shore,
For the Darkwater Monster
Had taken three more!

Two stolen already,
Now Mrs Patel,
And in the same flurry
The Ross boys, as well!

A helicopter hovered,
The coastguards were near,
And those on the beach
Gave their first hopeful cheer.

'Get out the flare guns,'
The coastguard chief said:
'You lads in the chopper,
Take aim at its head.'

A shower of flares
Gave the Monster a shock,
And it hurled its five captives
Up onto a rock.

It plunged underwater
In cascades of spray.
'I think you have done it!'
Cried Mrs Moray.

And those on the rock
Felt their hearts swell with hope,
As men in the chopper
Now lowered a rope.

But all hopes were dashed
And joy turned to dread,
As the **DARKWATER MONSTER**
Reared up its huge head…

THE MONSTER WAS BACK!

And a tentacle raked
Through the showers of foam.
It slithered and snaked…

And pulled down the chopper!
Numb with dismay,
None of those watching
Knew quite what to say.

Part Three

At last the chief spoke
To his crew, from the beach.
'S-stay clear of the Monster!
G-get out of its reach!'

Shouted Mrs Moray,
'I can see it's a blow,
But five of my school
Are still captives, you know!'

Just then a small aquaplane
Circled the bay:
'At last he is with us!'
Said Mrs Moray.

They quickly informed him
Of all they had seen.
'I wouldn't use flare guns,'
Said Mortimer Keene.

'I've got something better
To turn things around;
I'm going to attack
This sea monster with SOUND!'

He rode the wild surf
And the torrents of spray,
Chasing the Monster
Of Darkwater Bay.

'Hah! There's the creature,
I see where he's gone,'
Said Mortimer, switching
His SOUNDWHAMMER on.

An extremely low noise
Thundered under the sea,
Booming hideous sounds
In a menacing key.

The CRACKLES and BOOMS
Filled the Monster with dread.
It let go of the chopper
And suddenly fled!

In a flurry of foam
It shot out of the bay,
As Mortimer BOOMED it
Still further away.

Next, Mortimer twiddled
His dials to 'SLEEP' –
And 'Rock-a-bye Baby'
Flowed out through the deep…

Part Four

The team in the chopper
Burst open its door,
Got free of the wreckage
And swam for the shore.

The coastguards winched all
Of the five from the rock.
(Last came Mr Hart
Who had fainted from shock.)

Towels for the victims
Were brought out with speed,
And hot cups of tea
For those sorely in need.

'What news of the Monster?'
Enquired Mr Green.
'No problem at all,'
Replied Mortimer Keene.

'I stunned it with lullabies,'
Mortimer said.
'It's now snoozing away
On the deep ocean bed.'

'All the same, we must leave,'
Said Mrs Moray.
'And we'll call the Armed Forces,
It's risky to stay.'

They started to pack,
But there on the sand
Stood young Mr Bevan
With guidebook in hand:

'It says here quite clearly,
There may be ANOTHER.
I've just found a note on
The Monster's twin brother!'

'It's probably nonsense,
Enough for one day.
Come on, Mr Bevan,'
Said Mrs Moray.

'No more of the Monster,
We've children to teach.
Let's hurry on home –
We MUST leave the beach.'

There were sighs of relief,
And some shed a few tears
When the chief called his men
To give three hearty cheers.

For the kid in the aquaplane
Leaving the scene,
'And a flare-gun salute…

'For young Mortimer Keene!'

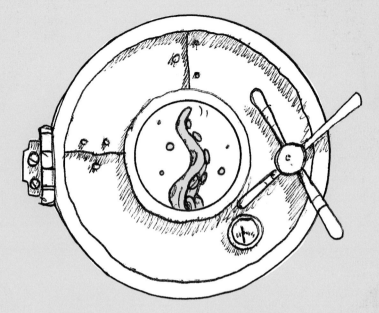

Following these events the armed
forces located the sleeping
Monster, which is now kept under
scrutiny in a high-security marina.
Mortimer Keene has been made
an honorary member of Her
Majesty's Coastguard.

Mortimer's
AQUAPLANE

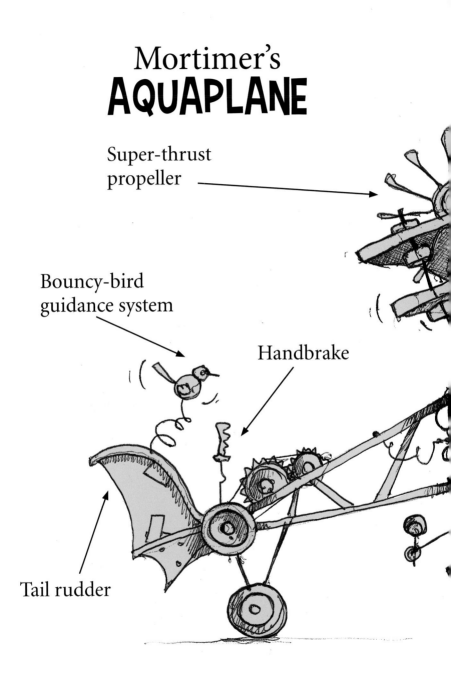

Super-thrust
propeller

Bouncy-bird
guidance system

Handbrake

Tail rudder

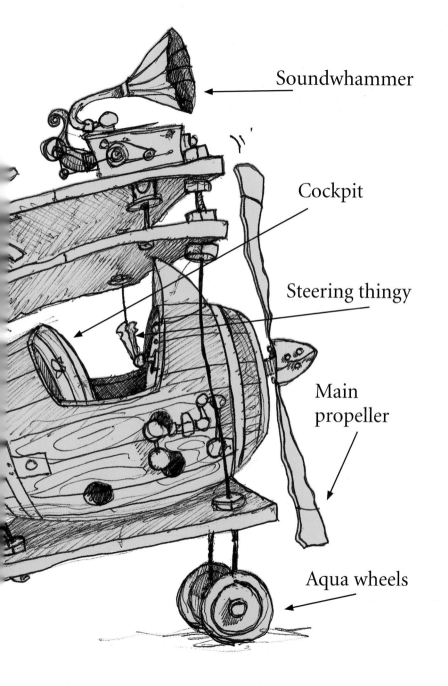

Soundwhammer

Cockpit

Steering thingy

Main
propeller

Aqua wheels

Mortimer's
SOUNDWHAMMER

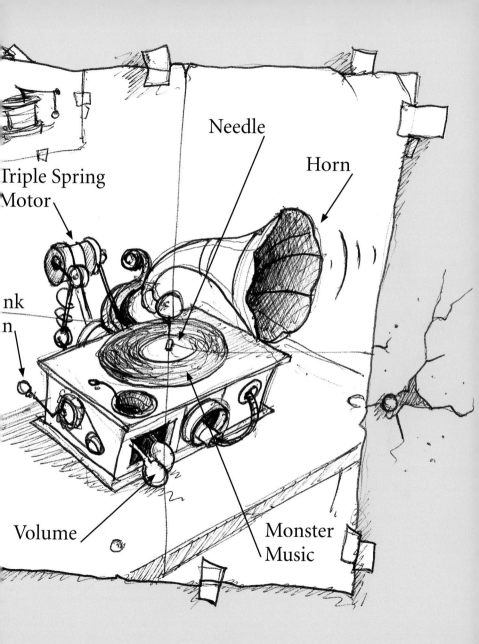

Needle

Horn

Triple Spring
Motor

nk
n

Volume

Monster
Music

SQUIDGY FACTS

The giant squid is a real-life creature that lives in the depths of the ocean. It can grow to 13 metres long (43 feet) – about as big as a bus! It is also supposed to be very smart.

The creature is very shy, but once in a while it may come to the surface. This may explain some sightings of sea monsters.

Giant squid have eight long arms and two even longer tentacles. Each tentacle has razor-toothed suckers, which are used for catching prey. The squid can shoot out its tentacles like lightning.

The enormous head has a mouth shaped like a beak. Each eye is as big as a football!

A-Z OF MURKY MONSTERS

ALGAE – type of plant that grows in water. Seaweed is a sort of algae and can grow and grow to form massive monster blobs.

BLOOP – in 1997 scientists detected a huge, ultra-low sound in the Pacific Ocean. They called it The Bloop and could not explain where it came from. Something to do with a monster?

CHAMP – lake monster said to live in Lake Champlain, between Canada and the United States.

DEEP-SEA GIANTS – creatures in the depths of the sea often grow much larger than those in the shallows.

EEK! – common response to sighting a sea monster.

FIJI MERMAIDS – fake mermaids often displayed by fairground showmen in past times.

GLOBSTER – weird mass of flesh that washes ashore and does not seem to come from any known animal.

HYDRA – legendary lake monster of the Ancient Greeks. It had many heads, and if you cut one off it grew two more!

ISSIE – mysterious monster often reported at Lake Ikeda in Japan.

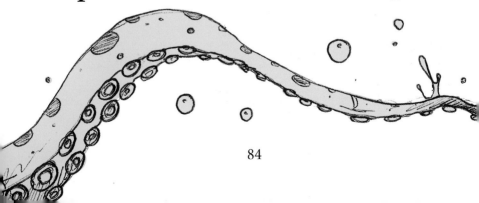

KRAKEN – massive sea creatures supposed to live off Greenland. Possibly based on sightings of giant squid.

LOCH NESS MONSTER – creature said to live in Loch Ness in Scotland.

MERMAIDS – sea creatures with the upper body of a woman and the tail of a fish.

NESSIE – popular name for the Loch Ness Monster.

OGOPOGO – snake like monster said to live in Canada's Okanagan Lake. All lakes with monsters are very, very deep.

PLESIOSAURUS – massive sea creature of dinosaur times, with a long neck and flippers.

QALUPALIK – legendary sea spirit of the Inuit people. Looks half-human, with green skin and long finger nails.

RUBBISH! – common response to tales of sea monsters.

SEA SERPENTS – monstrous sea snakes are reported in tales from all around the world.

TAHOE TESSIE – serpentine monster said to live in Lake Tahoe in the United States. Sometimes reported as a large black hump in the water.

URGH! – common response to seeing a globster.

VAMPIRE SQUID – this is a real creature: a squid whose eight arms are connected by a sinister black 'cloak' of webbing.

WHALES – may account for some reports of sea monsters. At 30 metres long (almost 100 feet), the blue whale is the largest animal known to have existed.

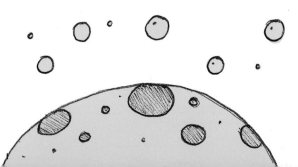

X OR PREDATOR X – name given to the biggest and fiercest of all the sea monsters of dinosaur times.

YACUMAMA – monster of South American legends. This giant water snake is said to live in the mouth of the River Amazon and suck up anything that comes within 100 paces.

ZOO – best place for the lot of them!

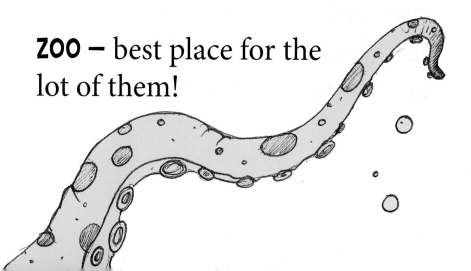

HANDPRINT SEA MONSTER

YOU WILL NEED

- Sheet of paper or card • Pen or pencil
- Scissors • Glue and other stuff

WHAT YOU DO

- Draw around your hand.
- Join up the lines at the wrist.
- Turn upside down. (No, don't *you* turn upside down! Turn the picture upside down, so the fingers dangle like legs.)

Draw big scary eyes, a mouth and anything else you like. Now cut out the monster. You can use glue to stick other stuff on your

monster and make it more impressive, such
as tassels of material, scaly shapes, sparkly
tinsel and so on.

TRUE OR FALSE?

1. Giant squid can change colour to fool their prey.

2. The tongue of a blue whale can weigh as much as an elephant.

3. The Nasty is the name of a legendary sea serpent said to haunt the English village of Nasty.

4. Giant cuttlefish have two hearts and yellow blood.

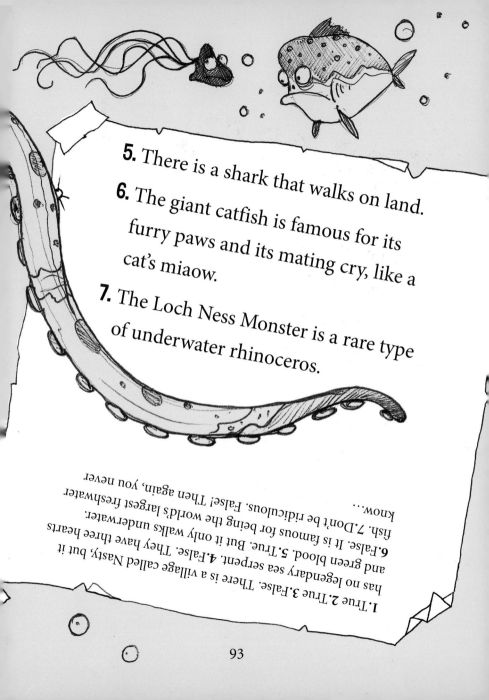

5. There is a shark that walks on land.

6. The giant catfish is famous for its furry paws and its mating cry, like a cat's miaow.

7. The Loch Ness Monster is a rare type of underwater rhinoceros.

1.True 2.True 3.False. There is a village called Nasty, but it has no legendary sea serpent. 4.False. They have three hearts and green blood. 5.True. But it only walks underwater. 6.False. It is famous for being the world's largest freshwater fish. 7.Don't be ridiculous. False! Then again, you never know…

Look out for these other **CRAZY** Mortimer books!

MORTIMER KEENE

ATTACK of the
SLIME!

Tim Healey and
Chris Mould

MORTIMER KEENE

GHOSTS
ON THE
LOOSE

Tim Healey and
Chris Mould